Oodles of Animals

CATERPILLAR

A caterpillar's future plan includes a butterfly wingspan.

Harcourt, Inc.   Orlando   Austin   New York   San Diego   London   Manufactured in China

BUTTERFLIES

AND MOTHS

Butterflies

and moths fly free.

They don't need

a suitcase or ID.

BUTTERFLY

Butterfly
wings
are angelic
things.

FLEA AND FLY

A fly can flee.
A flea can't fly.
But a flea can flee
and a fly can fly.

FLIES

Flies
on a log
might be lunch
for a frog.

BUMBLEBEE

Don't start a rumble
with a bumblebee,
or disgruntled
it will be.

MOSQUITO

Mosquito bites;
it gets plump.
All I get
is one big bump.

MOTHS

When moths
fly at night,
they like
porch lights.

DRAGONFLIES

Dragonflies
are fond
of a peaceful
pond.

BUGS

Ugly
bugs
don't get
hugs.

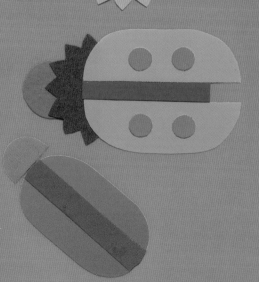

NEWT

A newt looks cute

in its polka-dot suit.

SALAMANDER

The shy

salamander

waits for dark

to meander.

FROG

In a bog,
a frog will wallow,
until he sees
a fly to swallow.

TOAD

A toad
is happy
to be
hoppy.

IGUANAS

Iguanas don't want
you in their face.
They prefer
to have their own spa[ce]

SNAKE

Sharing trails
with a snake
could be
a mistake.

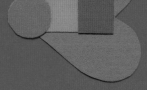

GECKO

A gecko climbs
on sticky toes
that cling to things
and don't let go.

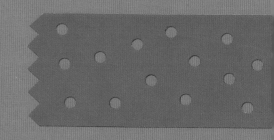

CROCODILE

Swimming and sunning,

a crocodile's happy.

But when he meets humans,

he tends to get snappy.

STARFISH AND SEA HORSES

Starfish don't shine;
they cannot.
And sea horses
don't gallop or trot.

CRAB

A crab
gets crabby
if you
get grabby.

SHRIMP

Shrimp ought
to be taught
not
to get caught.

LOBSTER

If you bother
a lobster,
it's a cinch
it will pinch.

FISH

Young fish families have some rules:

Look out for hooks, and stay in school.

STINGRAY

Stingray,
stay away!

SHARKS

Don't swim with sharks.
Quick! Head for the shore,
or you won't be swimming
any more.

ROOSTER

When a rooster crows
cock-a-doodle-doo,
does he wake up
the other roosters, too?

CHICKEN

If a chicken crossed
the road and rambled,
would the eggs she laid
be scrambled?

CARDINALS

Cardinals
are cheery
when days
are dreary.

PELICAN

In his pouch,
that's where the fish is,
so pelican can eat
whenever he wishes.

SWAN

A serene swan
silently floats.
Webbed feet paddle
her downy boat.

DUCK

A duck lays down
its sleepy head
upon its breast—
a feather bed.

PENGUINS

Penguins know
from birth
their wings won't fly
from Earth.

FLAMINGOS

Boy and girl

flamingos think

Mom's favorite color

must be pink.

SQUIRRELS

Greedy
squirrels feed
on bird-feeder
seed.

MOUSE

If cat nips at his tail,
a mouse better run,
or he'll be fast food
served up for one.

OPOSSUMS

Opossums' tails
are bare.
There's no
hair there!

BAT

A bat frown

is a smile

upside down.

RAT

Leave

a rat

where

it's at.

PORCUPINE

Porcupine quills flick,

and to you they will stick.

RACCOON

In a black mask,
he steals food we don't want
from a garbage can—
raccoon's restaurant!

SKUNK

If her tail's raised,
give a skunk room,
unless you like
pee-yoo perfume.

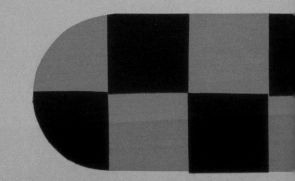

FOX

Dressed in fur and socks,

a fox trots.

Handsome from head to tail,

he likes himself—a lot.

BEAVER

Beaver teeth work
like a sharp saw.
When they find a tree,
they gnaw and gnaw and gnaw.

CAT

A cat

is a purr

wrapped up

in fur.

RABBIT

It's a rabbit ha[...]

to choose

fresh veggies

when she chew[...]

HAMSTER

A hamster
has soft fur,
but there's
no purr in her.

HEDGEHOG

A hedgehog is prickly and small in size,
like a pincushion with two beady eyes.

PIG

If you eat
like a pig,
sooner or later,
you will be big.

WOLF

A wolf downs his food
in a hurry.
If you hear him howl,
walk backward, and worry.

DOG

A dog's a true friend

from damp nose to tail's end.

LEOPARD AND LION

Leopard and lion paws

hide sharp claws.

DOLPHIN

A dolphin day begins
with leaps and spins.

SEAL

A seal

swims quicker

when wet

and slicker.

WALRUS

Walrus skin is rubbery,

and tusks rest on belly blubbery.

COW

Be sure you know
where and how
before you try
to milk a cow.

LLAMA

When llamas get a haircut,
they will look quite naked.
But you can knit a sweater
using their wool to make it.

MOUNTAIN GOAT

A goat must trust his hooves
to climb to the right spot,
because falling down a mountain—
that would hurt a lot.

BUFFALO

How do buffalo know
which way to roam?
Do they look at a map
before they leave home?

ELEPHANT

If an elephant
wants to dance,
say no.
You'd have a flat foot
if she stepped
on your toe.

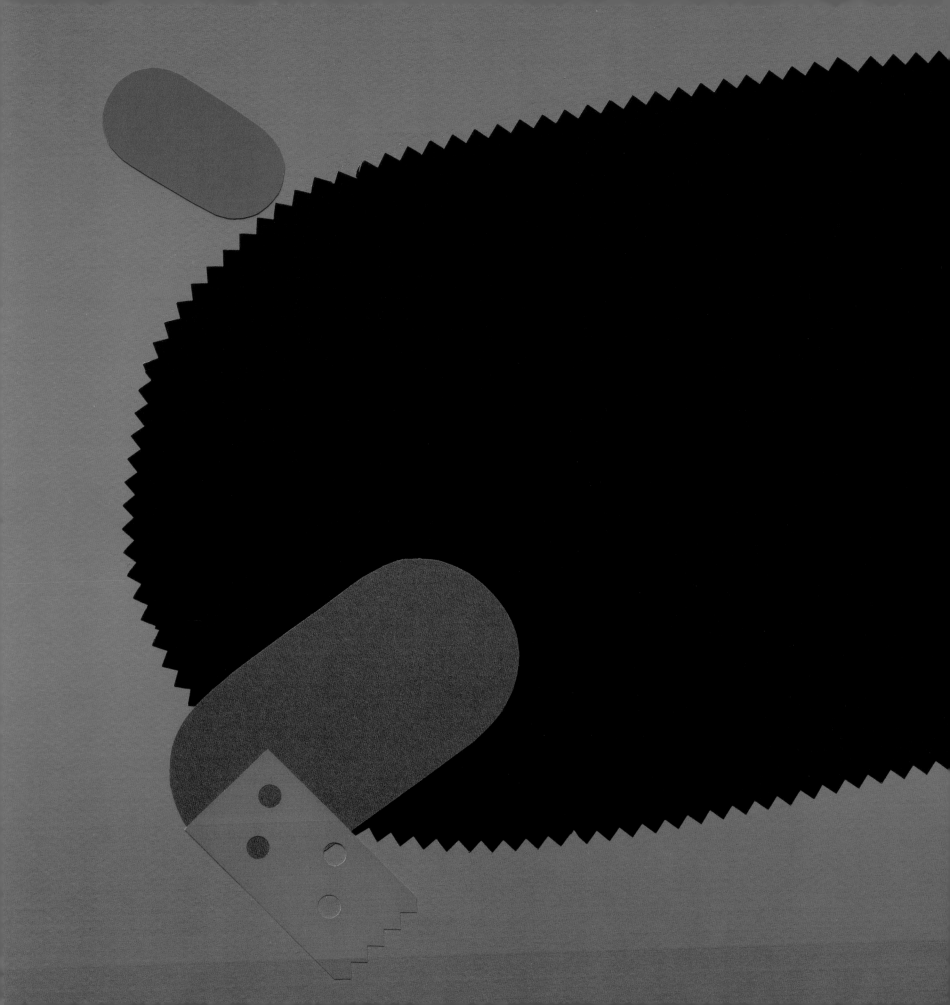

BEAR

If you go out walking,
and you see a bear,
tell your feet
to get out of there.

APE

Don't argue with an ape.

He's a brawny bruiser.

You may think you're clever,

but you'll be the loser.

MONKEY

If you take

a monkey to lunch,

feed him bananas,

and make it a bunch.

CHIMPANZEE

Furry hips, big ears and lips,
a chimp looks rather zany.
But inside, between those ears,
a chimpanzee is brainy.

For Dick and Shirley

www.HarcourtBooks.com

Library of Congress Cataloging-in-Publication Data
Ehlert, Lois.
Oodles of animals/Lois Ehlert.
p. cm.
Summary: Short, easy-to-read rhymes reveal what is unique about various
animals, from ape to wolf.
[1. Animals—Fiction.   2. Individuality—Fiction.   3. Stories in rhyme.]
I. Title.
PZ8.3.E29Ood   2008
[E]—dc22   2007017018
ISBN 978-0-15-206274-3

First edition

H G F E D C B A

AUTHOR'S NOTE

I've always been amazed at the diversity of animals.
As I began this book, I chose animals I liked, both
wild and tame, from different animal families.

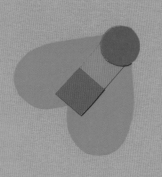

I used a variety of colored papers—along with scissors,
pinking shears, and a hole punch—and designed
each animal to show its distinctive features. As a
basic structure for the illustrations, I used nine
shapes: square, rectangle, triangle, circle, diamond,
half circle, oval, heart, and teardrop. If you ever see
a lion with blue hair and a red triangle for a nose, be
sure to let me know!